Adelbert J. D DeVillargennes

Reminiscences of Army Life

Under Napoleon Bonaparte

Adelbert J. D DeVillargennes

Reminiscences of Army Life
Under Napoleon Bonaparte

ISBN/EAN: 9783337349929

Printed in Europe, USA, Canada, Australia, Japan

Cover: Foto ©Andreas Hilbeck / pixelio.de

More available books at **www.hansebooks.com**

REMINISCENCES

OF ARMY LIFE

—UNDER—

Napoleon Bonaparte

BY

ADELBERT J. DOISY DE VILLARGENNES

Former Vice Consul of Italy at Cincinnati

———————————

CINCINNATI

ROBERT CLARKE & CO

1884

PREFACE.

Some six or seven years since, my father, at the request of a member of his family, undertook to write down a few recollections of his former career while serving in the army under Napoleon.

This work does not pretend to be a connected history of that period. As its title indicates, it is merely a series of *reminiscences* of events mostly within the experience of the writer; events which had impressed themselves more forcibly upon his mind than did other occurrences of equal or perhaps superior importance.

At the time of writing these memoirs, the author was about eighty-four years of age, but his memory was unimpaired in regard to all matters relating to the early period of his life. The strong grasp which the young mind had fastened upon the then present events had never released nor even slackened its hold, although the matured memory was dropping daily from its clasp, the more recent occurrences of life.

In the month of August, 1869, the one hundredth anniversary of the birth of Napoleon was celebrated with great enthusiasm by the French citizens of Detroit, Michigan. My father made the closing speech of the occasion; its peroration is here quoted as being a good exemplification of the ruling passion which ran through his life, and was strong even to the end:

"I never took any other oath of allegiance but that of fidelity to Napoleon and his dynasty; that oath I have kept; I shall keep it. I never uttered but one political exclamation, and it, I hope, will exhale itself with my dying breath:

'Vive l'Empereur Napoleon!'"

L. A. J. D. (Z. Z.)

REMINISCENCES OF ARMY LIFE
UNDER NAPOLEON I.

THE stirring events of the first decade in the present century were calculated to launch youth prematurely into the troubled ocean of man's life. I seem to have been destined to follow the tide. At the age of fifteen years I began the world on my own individuality. A tradition in our family asserted that one of its ancestors had been an admiral; this, possibly, together with the fact of my own adventurous disposition, influenced my parents' decision in regard to my future destiny, and it was settled that I should enter the navy.

In November, 1807, the Emperor Napoleon Bonaparte resolved to wrest Portugal from the domination of England, and sent for this purpose an expedition commanded by Junot. In the harbor of Lisbon was found a small

fleet, which the escaped family of Braganza
had no time to take away with them to
Brazil. The command of this squadron was
given to Commodore Magendie, a distant re-
lation of my mother, and he took me with
him as his secretary, although I was nomi-
nally enrolled as a novice on the books of
the Vasco de Gama, the flag-ship. During
the nine months, however, that our army
occupied Portugal, I was but three or four
times on board.

I may here state that my appointment as
secretary was due, not only to family interest,
but to my reputation among admiring friends
as an English scholar; for had I not gained a
premium at school for my extemporaneous
translation of a page of Goldsmith's "Vicar
of Wakefield?" Did I not glibly enough re-
peat from my book of dialogues such sen-
tences as the following, pronounced, too, as I
endeavor here to represent them: "Good
mor-naing, sair. Haou do you do? Zis is
bioutayfool oizer," etc.

After the battle of Vimeira and the con-

vention of Cintra, our army was conveyed
back to France in English vessels. But before leaving the Tagus, I must relate a comical
incident, which might, however, have had
serious consequences.

On the eve of sailing, General Laborde
invited several English army officers, from
whom he had received attention, to meet at
dinner some French officers who were on
board with him; as a compliment, he invited
likewise a navy officer named Garrott, who
acted then as Agent of the Transport Board.
This latter was a little, vulgar man, who,
whenever he had the opportunity, lost his
reason in his libations. Commodore Magendie and myself were also of the party, and
on account of my knowledge (?) of English I
was placed near Captain Garrott, to serve as
interpreter, if occasion offered. It was then the
3d of September, and the stern windows of
the cabin were left open on account of the heat.
The dinner passed on pleasantly, and friend
Garrott paid assiduous court to the bottles
within reach. When the fruit was laid on

the table, General Laborde rose, filled his
glass, and in a short, appropriate speech,
proposed the health of his Majesty, King
George III. The toast was drank with enthusiasm, the whole company standing. Then
an English officer (Colonel Haverfield, I believe) rose, and in courteous terms proposed the health of the Emperor Napoleon.
All glasses were cheerfully emptied, except
that of Garrott, who began to protest vo-
ciferously, in language wholly unbecoming a
gentleman, that he never would drink to the
health of "Boney." On the other side of me
was seated a French major of cavalry, Petit by
name, a man of Herculean size and power.
To this gentleman Captain Garrott now began to address his conversation, if such could
be called the volley of oaths and senseless
curses with which he seasoned his discourse,
until at last he roused the indignation of the
English officers. Major Petit had heretofore
remained imperturbable, but now, at an insulting gesture of Garrott, he rose, saying
coolly, "Gentlemen, be pleased to leave him

to me." Upon which he went to Garrott, seized him as he would a doll, by the collar and trousers, and walking to the window, balanced him for a moment, and then deliberately pitched him into the Tagus! Turning to the company: " Gentlemen," said he coolly, "if any one is dissatisfied, I am at his service." Several voices at once, accompanied by loud laughter, called out, "No, no! Well done! Served him right!" Meanwhile, poor Garrott was fished up by the crew of a boat moored astern of the ship, and returned all dripping to the cabin; apparently sobered, and giving no sign of displeasure at his strange visit to the Tagus.

Poor man! I should not speak lightly of him, for I owe him a debt of gratitude. Endowed with a sort of faculty or instinct, which enabled him to comprehend, or rather to guess the meaning of my language, he proclaimed me to all comers as a very satisfactory English scholar, and thus propped up my reputation, sadly shaken, if not wholly demolished, by an incident that occurred about this time.

A commissary in the English army having occasion to obtain some information from the commodore, called at our office, and his French being found unintelligible, he was referred to me. Our conversation must have been, to him at least, little edifying or satisfactory, for at last he concluded by saying in very bland tones: " My dear young friend, I wish you would talk French; I may perhaps make it out better than your English!" I was simple enough to rehearse this compliment among my acquaintances, and thereby drew upon myself sarcasm that tended not a little to crush whatever degree of conceit had been in me.

Shortly after my return to France, I was shipped on the frigate Pallas, where I passed my examination, and became a midshipman. On the night of April 11, 1809, the blockading English fleet sent fire-ships through ours, then at anchor. A few days after this event, I was surprised at receiving a commission as sub-lieutenant in the 26th regiment of infantry, then at Strasbourg, on its way to Germany, with orders to join it immediately. My father, without consulting me, and foreseeing quicker promotion in the army than in the navy, had obtained this commission for me. My regiment arrived at the island of Loban in time to share in the battle of Essling, May 22d, and in which, as my baptism of fire, I was wounded by the splinter of a shell.

In speaking of this, my first campaign, I shall abstain, for two reasons, from attempting to describe any of its varied engagements. First, I witnessed but few of its numerous skirmishes; second, I do not wish to resemble those who, on the plea that they were present at a battle, pretend to give an accurate account of the action; their very presence precludes their ability to present such a report. I speak, of course, of inferior officers only; they, indeed, can protray the evolutions of their own corps; the sudden passage of a battery of field artillery, or the momentary charge of a body of cavalry, etc. But the noise, the cloud of smoke, the agitation consequent upon each one obeying implicitly orders of which, perhaps, he does not understand the bearing; the extent of the field, sometimes, as at Wagram, covering miles; every circumstance, in short, tends to incapacitate the subaltern from filling faithfully the office of a reporter. Speaking for myself, I declare that after an engagement worth the appellation of a battle, I have invariably learned the particulars of it two or three days later from the bulletins of head-quarters.

Instead of venturing to discuss subjects beyond my power, I shall meet the object and the title of this narration better by relating two incidents which occurred in the course of this short campaign, premising that I did not witness either of them, but that they were the universal and uncontradicted subject of conversation in the army, though, for obvious reasons, publicity in the newspapers was suppressed.

After the battles of Eckmuhl and Ratisbon, a magnificent avenue leading to the latter city

had been totally ruined by the passage of up-
ward of two hundred thousand men. The
emperor ordered it to be repaired, and a company of infantry was posted at each extrem-
ity, with the express command not to allow
any one to enter it on horseback. General
Vandamme, as well known for his bravery as
for the extreme rudeness of his manners, presented himself on his horse at the entrance of
the avenue, and was proceeding further, when
the sentry on duty, a raw young recruit, came
forward and stated the orders he had received.
" General Vandamme passes anywhere !" exclaimed Vandamme; " get out of the way !"
On the soldier's appearing to insist, the general gave him a blow of his whip across the
face, cursing his impudence. The young lad,
intimidated, was about to yield, when the
captain who commanded at the post, and
who, walking about, had witnessed the scene,
rushed toward the sentry, snatched the musket violently out of his hands, and, running in
front of the general, leveled the piece at him,
exclaiming, " General, if you advance one

step more I will shoot you like a dog for daring to treat my sentry as you have done!" Vandamme, seeing at once whom he had to deal with, thought it best to comply, and withdrew, muttering a threat to revenge himself on the bold captain.

An opportunity soon presented itself. General Vandamme, being the temporary governor of Ratisbon, on visiting the different posts, recognized in the officer on duty at the main guard on the great square of the city the unlucky captain who had checkmated him at the avenue. The square was then swarming with lounging officers of all ranks. Vandamme took no apparent notice of his adversary, but having fully recognized him, went away without addressing him a word. Soon, however, profiting by the vicinity of a small crooked street, such as are almost all streets in Ratisbon, he suddenly re-appeared before the post. The sentry immediately called out the guard, according to regulations when the commanding general presents himself. The captain instantly rushed out with the guard, but so sudden and unexpected had been the second visit of the general that a few minutes elapsed before the ranks were formed and arms presented. Meanwhile, the general, standing motionless, had waited for this moment; then, giving vent to his brutal disposition, he assailed the unfortunate captain in the most opprobrious terms, telling him that he was fitter to drive a herd of hogs than to command soldiers, etc. By this time a crowd of officers had collected round the spot. The captain, during this painful scene, had sufficient control over himself to refrain from answering a single word. But, as soon as his post was relieved, he called on Marshal Oudinot, the commander of the staff, and, after relating the facts of the affair, demanded permission to challenge General Vandamme. The marshal, in rather severe tones, refused the request. On this the captain (his name was, I believe, Jollivet, 14th light infantry) did not hesitate a moment, but aware, as was all the army, how easy of access the emperor was, he at once determined on having direct recourse to his majesty. He accordingly repaired to the pavilion occupied by Napoleon, demanded and obtained an immediate audience, related in the fullest details both his interviews with General Vandamme, and concluded with a request for the same favor which he had vainly solicited from Oudinot. Napoleon, with his usual affability toward his inferiors, answered: "Sir, I sympathize with your feelings on this occasion; but you must feel that your demand is inadmissible. The general officers of the army are to be here to-morrow at twelve o'clock—come at the same hour. Meanwhile, I shall have strict inquiry made; and if, as I do not doubt, your version of the affair is quite correct, I shall require a suitable apology from General Vandamme to you."

Punctual to the hour, the captain attended the meeting, and modestly, from the inferiority of his rank, remained behind the circle formed round the emperor. The conversation, as on such ceremonious occasions, was confined to trivial subjects, and the company seemed preparing to take their leave, when our bold captain, elbowing his way through marshals and generals, stepped into the center of the circle, and fearlessly addressing the emperor, said : " Sire, you vouchsafed to promise me you would demand from General Vandamme, here present, some apology for the undeserved insults which he offered me. I come here in consequence of this promise."

Napoleon, without answering the captain, turned to Vaudamme, saying : " General, I have inquired into the facts of this disagreeable affair, and I find that you have most unwarrantably and outrageously insulted an officer who enjoys in his corps the highest character. You owe him a suitable apology, as public as your insult has been, and I insist on your making it here." " Sire," answered Vandamme, " I must regret having been carried away by passion in my addressing Captain Jollivet; but these gentlemen"—— " That's enough !" exclaimed the captain. " I am satisfied. Sire, I owe you more than my life. I thank your majesty." He could say no more; emotion had stifled his voice; he bowed and retired.

I have not heard what his subsequent career may have been.

It frequently happened that sudden acclamations of " Vive l'Empereur!" stirred the humors of our bivouac fires. This often occurred from the enthusiasm of the soldiers at the recital of some trait in the life of their idolized chief. The first outpouring of such a feeling witnessed by me was occasioned by the animated account of the foregoing incident by a sergeant to a large concourse of soldiers. The strict sense of justice; the generosity of Napoleon toward those who had served well, or toward the families of those who had fallen; his paternal attention to those in hospitals; his severe surveillance over the conduct of contractors for the supply of the troops; the commanding influence which he unaffectedly exerted over his most distinguished generals; all these aroused the enthusiasm of our soldiers at the mere recital of some agreeable trait in the acts of their idol.

I feel a certain reluctance in relating the second incident alluded to above, as it affects

a character for which I profess and entertain
the highest respect: that of a French officer.
But there are in all armies a few individuals
unworthy of the epaulets which they wear;
and the publicity given to the unmasking
and punishing the man who has disgraced his
rank is a lesson of public morals which may
have more than one useful application.

While a part of the army was at Passau, at
the confluence of the river Inn with the Danube, a major in the artillery of the Imperial
Guard (I shall suppress his name) had ac-
quired a most detestable notoriety by the
number of duels, by him styled successful,
which he had fought. His skill with sword
or pistol, as well as his insolence, had become
proverbial, and his comrades had nicknamed
him " Le grand diable." One day, at a coffee
house much frequented by officers, two captains
in the 65th of the Line had been there playing
a game of billiards. One of them, having
momentarily left the room, his friend was
awaiting him, standing near the table. At
this moment in stepped the major, accom-

panied by two friends. Approaching the table he took up the balls, and was proceeding to arrange them anew when the absent gentleman returned and interposed, stating in polite terms that the table was engaged, as he and his friend were then in the midst of a game. "I insist," exclaimed the major, "that the table is not engaged when people are not actually playing!" The captain answered in a few angry words, when the major, seizing and placing one of the balls before him, vociferated, "I tell you that I have a right to the table, and let me see who will presume to touch this ball." The captain, without replying, took up a cue, and coolly drove the ball before him. On this, the major struck a violent blow in the face of his antagonist. Several officers rushed forward to interpose, but the captain, anticipating them, addressed the major in something like the following terms: "Sir, you have mortally insulted me, and I shall have satisfaction; but on equal terms, for I shall not allow you to kill me as you boast having done so many others. I hold in my hand a few coins: name you odd or even. If you guess right you will shoot me; but if you miss I shall certainly blow out your brains, for one of us must not leave this room alive." So saying, he withdrew his closed hand from his pocket, exclaiming, "Now, call out!" Without appearing much disturbed, the major sung out, "Even!" The captain then laid his open hand on the table, saying to the friends of the major, "Gentlemen, be pleased to count." There were *seven* Napoleons displayed to the view of all.

The captain turned to the friend with whom he had been playing, and desired him aloud to go to his lodging and bring him his pistols, which were loaded. He departed, and the captain locked the door after him, putting the key in his pocket. The persons present, about twenty in number, walked silently about the room, awaiting the sequel of this exciting scene. The messenger returned, handed the pistols to his friend, who forthwith stepped up to the major, and presented the weapon to his face with the words, "Are you ready?" The

two friends of the major now wished to interpose their mediation, which the captain firmly
declined to permit; till, finally, on their observ-
ing that the major was paymaster to his corps,
and had some important papers to settle, it
was agreed that he should be allowed to with-
draw for the space of half an hour; his friends,
meanwhile, remaining as guarantees for his
return. This was done, and in the meantime
the two gentlemen, renewing their kind endeavors, said almost jocularly: "But surely,
captain, you do not intend to avail yourself
of your right, and shoot him?" "But I as-
suredly *do* intend it," retorted the captain.
"I shall, however, for your sakes, gentlemen,
leave him one other alternative, which will be
that he will leap out of this window into the
street; if he decline to avail himself of this
chance, I shall certainly make a hole in him."

Half an hour—a whole hour elapsed—
and the *Grand Diable* had not re-appeared.
The only information obtained, two or three
days later, was that on the day of the above
events, he had been seen passing beyond the

outposts; thus giving the sad, and I rejoice to add, the solitary instance of a French officer deserting to the enemy; if I except the infamous treason of Bourmont, on the eve o. Waterloo.

About the same time a ludicrous incident occurred, which occasioned a good deal of merriment in the army. I relate it as exhibiting the artless and implicit confidence which the soldiers reposed in the emperor's word, and also in his power.

Some depredations having been committed in the country by our troops, Napoleon issued an order of the day, denouncing severe penalties upon the perpetrators of such outrages, and, at the same time, promising that all losses arising from such cases, on being satisfactorily proved, should be paid by the intendent general of the army.

A marching company of infantry had been quartered for the night in a large inn, situated in a suburb of the ancient town of Donauwerth, on the Danube; and the men rejoiced at being assigned as their dormitory an immense

barn, filled with hay and other provender. ·
During the night the captain's attention was
aroused by a loud altercation which proceeded
from the barn, and thither he hastily repaired.
He arrived in time to hear the conclusion,
which was somewhat as follows :   "Oh !" mis-
ter soldier ! in the name of all the saints !"
exclaimed in broken French, and in a most
dolorous tone of voice, the proprietor of the
inn, "I humbly beg you will not go on smok-
ing there; you may set my poor property on
fire, and still worse, burn the whole city of
Donauwerth !"   " Well !" roared out the soldier, "what of that, you old fool?   Have you
not read the emperor's order of the day, pla-
carded on all the walls of the town?   Why,
if I burn it, they'll pay it to you, your old
city !"

Napoleon, before the public, thought it de-
sirable to appear stern, even to severity; but,
with his friends, such as Cambacérès, Murat,
Caulaincourt, Duroc, and Savary, he yielded
to his natural affability, and even, sometimes,
indulged in a good-natured jest or pleasantry.

After the conclusion of the campaign of Wagram, the emperor returned to France. He was met on the bridge of the Rhine by an immense concourse of people, and a deputation headed by M. de Pontécoulant, prefect of the department of Bas-Rhine, and one of the most eminent among the civilians of this epoch.

The prefect had carefully prepared an address suited to the occasion; but the excitement of the moment, the display of military pomp, the surrounding staff, perhaps also some of that uncontrollable feeling at sight of the emperor which I had myself experienced, and which at this time was shared by nearly the whole of France: all these causes combined produced so powerful an effect on M. de Pontécoulant that he suddenly totally forgot his intended speech. However, in hopes that once the ice broken, he might recover his treacherous memory, he ventured to begin in tremulous accents: "Sire, your faithful subjects of the city of Strasbourg are so happy at seeing you again that—that—Sire, your faithful sub-

jects are so happy that"— "Oh! yes!" the
the emperor exclaimed, at the same time
shaking cordially the dismayed prefect by the
hand, "My friend, M de Pontécoulant, and
the kind citizens of Strasbourg are so happy
to see me that they *can not express their joy!*"

On one occasion, Savary, the minister of
police, gave notice to the emperor of an in-
dividual who had repeatedly solicited an audience of his majesty. He had been refused admittance, being an absolute stranger, but he
was still, at that moment, sitting on the stair-
case of the Tuileries. Napoleon desired his
immediate admittance, upon which he was
introduced by Savary. Napoleon asked the
man his business. "Sire," was the reply,
"the communication I have to make is of
such a nature that to your majesty alone I
can intrust it." The emperor then desired
Savary to leave the room, and resumed his
writing. A few minutes passed, and the
stranger, remaining silent, Napoleon exclaimed, with some irritation, "Well, why don't
you speak?" "Sire," answered the man, "as I

stated before, I can not speak unless to your majesty alone." The emperor turned around, and seeing Savary still standing near the door of the apartment, reitererated in a stern voice the order to leave the room. Savary hastily answered: " I will not, Sire. This fellow has a villainous physiognomy; and besides, from information I have procured, I find he is a Corsican; I do not trust him." " Ah! indeed!" said the emperor, with a smile; "a Corsican, is he? Well, so am I. Leave us instantly." The stranger remained closeted for a considerable time with Napoleon; and conjecture itself has never been able to ascertain who he was or the character of his errand. This incident is more than alluded to in the "Mémoires de Savary," but not mentioned in the "Mémorial de St. Hélène."

The campaign being ended, we went by short stages through the greater part of Germany, and through a large part of France, diagonally, having recrossed the Rhine at Dusseldorf, and scarcely halting for one day, until we reached Bayonne. There we remained four days, to renew our arms and accoutrements, and to receive recruits, having left four hundred of our men buried in German soil. We re-entered Spain on the 6th day of October, 1809, as a part of the corps commanded by Marshal Ney.

Here, what a contrast awaited even those of us who had previously visited Iberia. To the sauerkraut, the noodles, and the white beer, which we had abundantly enjoyed in Bavaria, and scantily in Austria, had succeeded, in our passage through France, the usual rations of rather poor meat, *pain de munition, id est,* bread made half of rye flour and half of wheat and bran; the whole seasoned with as much cold water as the men were inclined to imbibe. Still, we were then on our native soil, and the hospitable inhabitants, although already taxed by the incessant passage of numerous armies, exerted themselves to the utmost to evince their sympathy with the men who had fought abroad the battles of the fatherland.

Here in Spain, for food, a solid, massive

bread, composed of maize, with a small proportion of wheaten flour; garvanzos, tomatoes, pimentos, a rare distribution of skinny, meager goats' flesh, accompanied by a scanty allowance of *tolerably* good wine, but so saturated with the taste and odor of the goatskins in which it had been transported that the men at first could scarcely be induced to taste it—such, generally, was the fare that awaited us in Spain—happy, if even this could always be available.

The climate brought us another disappointment. I, like many others, had formerly visited Spain in summer only, and we represented the country as being warm indeed, but heavenly in its generally pure atmosphere, its balmy zephyrs, and its luxuriant, healthy soil. War, it must be remembered, had not at that time devastated the country in which we were, as yet, generally regarded as friends, and we had left it with minds fully disposed to describe *couleur de rose* every thing connected with Spain. We very soon had to admit a strange contrast to our fond anticipations.

In some respects, however, our people were not disappointed; and especially in the language of the country. This so much resembled their own that they were enabled readily to guess, if not fully to comprehend, its meaning; they were aided also by the intelligent, earnest gestures, which were never-failing accompaniments of every word uttered.

The common character of the Spaniards was likewise strikingly agreeable. The long occupation of Spain, combined with native manners derived from their Gothic ancestors, the Moors, then the most civilized people on the globe, and the blind subserviency of the people to the double tyranny of the court and the clergy, had stamped the personality of the middle classes, as well as that of the peasantry and of the working classes, with a submissive cast of deportment, which was by no means indicative of servile submission, but rather of a respectful, though distant regard; for, in their conduct toward their superiors, I have often noticed a certain degree of haughtiness which betrayed an origin of Moorish nobility.

But the temperature of the country very soon led the new-comers to accuse of optimism those of us who had given so flaming an account of the climate. When engaged in the defiles of the Guadarrama, we happened to be overtaken by a furious snowstorm, and that so suddenly that we were not fully prepared for winter. My company was quartered in a small village, the name of which I shall not forget, for there I encountered the severest cold I ever experienced anywhere. It was called Villalba, within a short distance of the famed castle of San Ildefonso, and of La Granza (the barn), the favorite residence of several Spanish monarchs.

It does not enter into the plan of this narrative to attempt topographical descriptions, yet I can not pass on without giving a brief account of a monument which appeared to me as stupendous, regarded as a work of art,

as those creations of Divine power, the Falls
of Niagara, or the snow-capped dome of
Mont Blanc. I allude to the aqueduct, which,
after traversing ten miles of hill and vale,
supplies San Ildefonso and Segovia with
water. This work, unique in its grandeur,
has been attributed to Trajan, but the simple
natives doubt such an origin, and very generally affirm that the aqueduct has always existed, and was not constructed by human
hands. Imagine a structure composed of two
stone canals superposed with an interval of
some twenty feet, and composed in their
whole course of ten miles of enormous blocks
of granite, so admirably fitted to each other,
that without a particle of cement, not a drop
of water can escape, and you may form some
conception of the aqueduct of Segovia.

From old Castile we went through Madrid
and New Castile to Estremadura; here nothing occurred which could tally with the object
of this memoir. However, I may not omit
stating an observation which struck us all,
and, if well founded, is an anomaly peculiar to

Spain, in contradistinction to other nations. In France, in Germany, in England, you may distinguish the natives of the several provinces by some intonations or peculiar *patois*, but in general characteristics they are still essentially French, German, English. In Spain you may at once discern perceptible differences, not so much in language as in manner, complexion, and customs. To the lively, smart manners, the spirited disposition of the Arragonese, to the affected pride of the inhabitants of Madrid, and the wretched misery of the country parts of old Castile, succeeded in Estremadura a listless sort of apathy, a gravity of deportment, which might be ascribed less to physical constitution than to the isolation in which the province was left by the want of roads and other means of communication with foreign countries, or even with neighboring provinces. Yet the people are reasonably proud, deriving, as I said, this trait from their former rulers, the civilized Moors; and in the midst of poverty to which they seem reconciled, they make excellent soldiers. The best horsemen in the Spanish army are natives of Estremadura.

At Truxillo, I witnessed that darling spectacle of Spaniards, a bull fight. I was disappointed in the expectations raised previously by hearsay or by written accounts. I saw nothing here but wretched panic-struck bulls, maimed or butchered by awkward matadors, and two miserable horses gored by the bulls.

At Merida, where we were quartered, we found a town of few inhabitants, but of large extent, and possessing majestic tokens of ancient splendor in the numerous monuments left by the Romans, at the time of their occupation.

Our corps now returned northward to the province of Leon, and there accident occasioned the most active service I had as yet experienced. The head-quarters of our division was at Salamanca. Whilst in that city, I was ordered, with a section of my company, to escort a small convoy to the town of Toro. There, the feeble garrison being deemed insufficient to resist the numerous guerillas with which it was surrounded, I was detained, *nolens volens*, by the general commanding, and employed during the month of January in hunting for guerillas, generally with little success; they were too nimble and also too well acquainted with the country. There was no question of a regular engagement, but now and then, over hedges or other inclosures, we were suddenly assailed with a volley of musketry, and our only satisfaction was to see a dozen men running full speed in a direction in which it would have been madness to follow. I lost four men in one of these ambuscades.

On my return to Salamanca, I found that my regiment had gone to share in the siege of Cindad Rodrigo; and again I was detained by General Thirbauch, the chief of the staff, for nearly the same reasons that had caused my detention at Toro; the only difference was, that in addition to chasing the guerillas, and protecting communications on the roads to Toro and Valladolid, I had to levy contributions of provisions and forage through a district of several leagues in extent. According to orders, I always delivered to the people levied upon a receipt, forming a draft on the intendant of the army, but I can not assert that these drafts were very punctually honored. This service was the most agreeable I ever had in the army. In the first instance, I was, when on special duty, general-in-chief of my detachment; obliged to obey orders as to the object of the expedition, but with absolute *carte blanche* as to the details. Besides, my detachment had been doubled, by receiving into it all men leaving the hospital. From the same source, I received all the accoutrements I wanted. As to food, we took care of that in the villages that we visited, although we never slept in one for fear of being surprised by guerillas, but uniformly camped out of town. My men carried no money, and thus the guerillas, knowing that no booty was to be obtained from them except the contents of their cartridge-boxes, and this in a manner not altogether pleasant, very seldom attacked us.

Here it strikes me that the reader may justly be surprised that so independent a service as that described above should have been intrusted to the hands of such a youngster as I was. This would at once be understood by those familiar with the French army at that time, but here demands some explanation.

In England, the honor grades of officers, with very few exceptions, are filled up by purchase, and afterwards permit exchanging from one corps to another, with little or no difficulty. In Germany, the sons of nobles, or of persons high in office, alone enjoy the privilege of entering the army as officers; it was so, at least, at the time of which I write. Quite different was the system followed in France. All private soldiers, whose conduct and ability entitled them to this distinction, were recommended by the council of administration of their respective regiments, then approved by the minister of war, and finally nominated by the emperor to the rank of *sous-lieutenant* (corresponding to the title of

ensign in England and to that of second
lieutenant in the United States). A few mid-
shipmen were transferred from the navy to
this rank in the army. But by far the greater
number of our *sous-lieutenants* had been pu-
pils of the military school at Fontainebleau,
and later at Saint Cyr. At the period of
this narrative, education was at a very low
ebb indeed throughout France, except in the
cities, where good schools were well sup-
ported. But in the country parts, from which
we received nine-tenths of our recruits, the
native intelligence of the people rendered less
baneful the almost total absence of literary
instruction. Hence, incredible as it may appear, in a company of one hundred and
twenty-one men, I have, excluding sergeants
and corporals, counted only eight men capa-
ble of reading or writing. From this strange
state of ignorance arose a curious result,
peculiar, I believe, to the French army, and
pregnant with remarkable consequences. The
young men in the ranks had, when leaving
home, left earnest requests for news to be

forwarded to them by letters written by the priest or the school-master of their respective villages. Such letters, after reaching the regiment, had to be read and answered, but by whom ? for they sometimes contained information either ludicrous or susceptible of bringing a blush to the cheek of the recipient. To communicate such correspondence to those of their comrades learned in the alphabet might have exposed them to the jeers and perhaps the contempt of their fellow soldiers ; to apply to field officers, or even to captains, would have been too wide a leap over the chasm separating the ranks; there remained one resource—the *sous-lieutenants.* These were nearly of an age with the recruits, and sufficiently superior in rank to remove the fear of indiscretion among the soldiers; hence, the *sous-lieutenant,* or sometimes the first lieutenant of each company, became the amanuensis, and necessarily the intimate confidant of the great majority of his men. It was thus, that before I was twenty years of age, I had become acquainted with the special and family affairs of upwards of fifty men, and had written for them several wills, powers of attorney to their relatives, or vows of eternal love to their sweethearts. The consequences may be anticipated. The young officers became seriously interested in the welfare of their men; the latter could hardly find opportunities enough to evince their ardent attachment for their youthful protectors. Many a field officer was left for a time, wounded on the field, for a sous-lieutenant *must* first be removed out of the fire. In times of scarcity, and we experienced many such, as I may have occasion to state hereafter, I had more than once the satisfaction of sharing with my captain, or the major of the battalion, bread, tobacco, eggs, meat, poultry, rabbits, wine, etc.; the fruits of some successful marauding of my men. The remarkable progress of education within the last fifty years leads me to surmise, that with the cause the effect has vanished, and thus put an end to the system in question.

An incident which occurred in the month

of June, 1810, forming rather a prominent event in my army life, I can scarcely omit the mention of it in these *reminiscences* of my former career.

The band of guerillas commanded by Don Julian Sanchez, in the west, had not an equal in Spain, with the exception of the one in the north, directed by the celebrated Mina. Don Julian had for his most zealous lieutenant a young man, who, for some motive of private revenge, rather than patriotism, had forsaken his profession of lawyer to raise a band of guerillas, whom he dressed in French uniforms; for he was said to have made a vow not to spare the life of any French soldier who should fall into his hands.

One evening I arrived at Salamanca with a supply of provisions, and very tired, after a long march under a midsummer sun. My report being made, I returned to the convent, the great refectory of which was always reserved for my detachment; saw my men all sound asleep on their straw, and lay down myself, rejoicing in the idea of making a night of it. About

eleven o'clock my sentry awoke me, introducing an orderly, who brought a command to at-
tend immediately at head-quarters, on the great
square of the city.   I can not speak very flat-
teringly of the good grace with which I obeyed
this unseasonable infringement of my repose,
but obey I must, and did.   General Thiébault
was-writing at his desk when I made my appearance, and his first words were: "How many
men have you now?"   "Eighty-four, Sir."
"Well," he continued, "you shall start immediately with your whole detachment, and not
stop until you reach the village called Los
Pavones."   "Sir!" I exclaimed, involuntarily,
"Los Pavones is eleven Spanish leagues (about
forty English miles) from this, and my men
are nearly used up with the last ten days'
march in the mountains, and "— "Enough,"
said the general, sternly.   "Don Aguilar is
ill in the priest's house at Los Pavones; the
man whom you see there sitting in the corner
is a spy, who has already done good service,
and who undertakes to conduct you to the
very house."

The general need not have said so much; the very name of Aguilar struck through my whole being a chord which would have vibrated in the heart of the most apathetic man in the army. I eagerly undertook the mission, received a few more instructions on the subject, and reflecting that it would be impossible to reach my destination in less than ten hours, and that to attempt the capture in daylight would insure its failure, I took upon myself to let my men continue their sleep a couple of hours more, and at two o'clock started, keeping a strict guard on the spy, who accompanied us.

At four o'clock in the afternoon of the next day, we arrived within two leagues of Los Pavones. A large vineyard appearing at a short distance from the road, I marched my men into it, made them lie down, with strict injunctions not to raise their heads, and upon this welcome recommendation, they were all soon sound asleep.

At dusk, under a gentle shower of rain, we started again, and reached our destination between ten and eleven o'clock. The spy brought us faithfully to the door of the priest's house. Leaving the sergeant to watch in front, I went with a part of my men to place sentinels in a garden which seemed to surround the place. During my short absence, a servant-girl happened to come out with a pail of water, which she was probably about to empty into the street. My sergeant had the presence of mind to throw his arm around the girl's face, thus effectually preventing any noise on her part. I returned at this moment and the door being half open, I went in, accompanied by a dozen men. On entering the hall, I saw a light issuing from an apartment, the door of which was wide open. To this I proceeded, securing in my hand a pocket pistol, which had been given me by my brother, and which had accompanied me in all my expeditions. Having little doubt of being near the successful issue of the adventure, I plunged at once into the room, and beheld—not Aguilar, indeed, but a venerable old man, sitting up in bed, and reading by the light of a lamp. At sight

of me and my men, he uttered an exclamation
of terror, which I soon silenced. After he
had somewhat recovered, I learned from him
that Aguilar was, indeed, in the house, where
he had been compelled to receive him; that
he was now in an apartment at the end of the
hall, and, as he verily believed, in a dying
state. To the room thus indicated, we instantly repaired; the door was locked inside,
but three or four stout men soon removed this
obstacle. At this moment, there was a great
crash in the room, and two shots fired outside.
We rushed in, and saw through the feeble
obscurity of a June night, a bed on the right
hand side of the room. We threw ourselves
precipitately on this bed, and called loudly for
a light. I felt no movement under me, but
my hair was suddenly grasped most violently,
which caused me to undergo intolerable pain.
A light was finally brought in, and showed
the singular spectacle of six men overlaying a
motionless body, while one of these men, myself, was held most unmercifully by the hair
and throat, in the hands of—my own sergeant!

Aguilar had not fainted, although laboring under a heavy fever, but he was taken by surprise, and rendered absolutely powerless.

The noise we had heard was occasioned by the hasty opening of a window and two shots from my men, by which one of Aguilar's attendants had been killed on the spot; the other escaped. Two loaded pistols were on a table in the middle of the room and two helmets belonging to French dragoons.

We found in the stable a couple of excellent horses fully equipped. After having regaled my men with whatever the house afforded, and taken some hours' rest, we bound Aguilar, placed him in a sort of buggy belonging to the priest, and made the latter mount his mule to accompany us. This proceeding was not accomplished without the most pitiful lamentations from the poor old man; for, by an order of the day, to which the utmost publicity had been given, any person receiving a guerrilla into his house was liable to capital punishment. I assured him that I would see

him safe from any penalty, but that my orders to bring him with me were imperative.

Our march was uninterrupted by accident,
and we reached Salamanca about eight o'clock
the next evening. I rode one of the horses
we had captured, and during the march used
my utmost Spanish eloquence to convey some
comfort to the heart of my unhappy prisoner,
assuring him that the worst he had to expect
was to be sent as a prisoner of war to France,
where the best treatment awaited him. But
all my endeavors were vain; either Aguilar
did not understand me, or he disdained to
answer, but he observed throughout an ob-
stinate and contemptuous silence, and utterly
refused to accept any nourishment, with the
exception of two glasses of lemonade.

In coming down to see the prisoners, General Thiébault asked for the priest. I pointed
to him, where he sat trembling on his mule to
the left of the detachment, but told the general that I was certain the old man had acted
under compulsion, and that, besides, I had
given my word that he should be set at liberty

on our arrival. "You were very wrong to promise such a thing," was the answer, "but it is nearly dark; send him off quietly. I'll not see him." The poor priest did not need much explanation; he testified his satisfaction by plying the flanks of his mule vigorously with his heels, and soon disappeared.

Two days later, my unhappy prisoner was tried by court-martial, convicted by the testimony of some of his own countrymen, of barbarous murders committed upon French soldiers, and hung on the main square of Salamanca. He had to be carried, already half dead, to the place of execution; I did not, could not witness the last scene, though I was present at the trial.

A few days after, I obtained leave to rejoin my regiment at Ciudad Rodrigo, and thence to the short siege of Almeida. The army, which now took the denomination of "Army of Portugal," was commanded by Marshal Masséna, Prince of Essling. It numbered fifty-four thousand men, and reckoned among its chief officers such men as Ney, Junot,

Loison, Reille, and other distinguished military characters.

Almeida, after the explosion of its principal magazine, surrendered; an indecisive engagement took place in its vicinity, and the English army commenced its retreat towards Lisbon. We soon followed, having first provided each soldier with five days' provisions; for Lord Wellington had issued a proclamation, inviting the Portuguese to follow his army, taking away all they could carry, and burning or destroying the rest. The inhabitants very generally complied, and thus set an example, which, three years later, was followed by the Russians at Moscow.

Here then we had before us a march of two hundred miles, across a mountainous country, nearly deserted by its population, and bare of all kinds of supplies. The men, overloaded with their accoutrements, their arms, their sixty rounds of cartridges, and their five days' rations of provisions, soon threw away a part of the latter, and we had barely reached Guarda before scarcity

began to be sensibly felt. The enemy continued their retreat, making no stand until at
Busaco, September 27, 1810, the sixth corps,
to which my regiment belonged, found itself
ten miles in advance of the fourth corps, with
the commander-in-chief, and two miles in advance of the second corps, under the command of General Reille. The enemy must
have been well aware of this faulty disposition; for, instead of continuing their retreat,
they had halted at Busaco, and the first thing
we perceived, on arriving, was a battery of
eight guns frowning on an eminence commanding the village. Marshal Ney, the commander of our corps, came to reconnoiter the
position, and with his usual impetuosity, led
our regiment to the village, which the English
soon abandoned, and then sent us, under General Simon, to storm the battery. We did so,
and at first did not meet with any serious
rebuff. Suddenly, however, from three sides
of the hill, appeared masses of infantry, in
numbers sufficient to annihilate our poor 26th
regiment. In less time than I can describe it,

the tide of affairs changed wofully. General Simon was knocked off his horse, with a ball in his neck, and left on the field for dead, our colonel (Barrère, brother of the notorious Jacobin) was killed, as well as three of our majors, eight captains, four lieutenants, and about four hundred rank and file. A panic ensued among us, and contrary to those heroes who boast of never having turned their backs to the enemy, I must confess that on the order to retreat, given by our remaining major (later our excellent colonel, Ferry by name), we did not wait for an additional command of *quick step*, but showed our discrimination between going *up* and coming *down* hill. I, for one, must confess that I never appreciated more fully the good sense of that saying of Napoleon, "L'art de la guerre est dans les jambes, autant que dans la tête."[1] Our colors were saved, and a considerable promotion took place in the regiment, now much reduced in numbers, so that we accepted our discomfiture

---

[1] "The art of war is in the legs as much as in the head."

philosophically enough; though bitter reflec-
tions were made on the reckless manner in
which Marshal Ney had sacrificed our corps.
His rash conduct highly incensed the Prince
of Essling, and the coolness which had for
some time been suspected to exist between
the two chiefs soon became apparent to the
army.

The southward march of both armies continued, without any other serious conflict,
till, reaching the strong position of Torres
Vedras, the enemy came to a full stand, and
Masséna was so struck with the natural
strength of the heights that he devoted four
days to a careful study of the approaches, and
finally concluded on the inexpediency of storm-
ing them. Meanwhile, Wellington, profiting
by our hesitation, procured from Lisbon a
fleet, as well as a vast force of artillery, with
which he covered all available points, thus
rendering his lines really impregnable. Marshal Ney, who on our arrival, had strongly recommended an immediate attack, had the indiscretion to blame publicly the inopportune de-

lay of his superior, hinting that the latter was no longer the Masséna of 1796, and that, had we attacked at once, we might almost with ease, have annihilated the English army. Ney was probably right in his opinion, but his giving vent to it in angry and indiscreet words, sure to be repeated, widened the unhappy breach between the marshals, and had an indirect effect on the issue of the campaign.

Entrenched camps were soon established in various directions; that of our brigade was on the road to Santarem. The rainy season had begun; we had no stores, and no possibility of communication with Spain; food, forage, clothing, all necessaries, even to a sufficiency of ammunition, were wofully scarce, and to prevent starvation, the army was soon reduced to the necessity of marauding. This was carried on by organized parties detached from each regiment, and sent to parts of the country not occupied by either of the belligerents. Such expeditions, unavoidable as they were, soon proved of little avail, and were actually injurious to discipline. Parties, commanded by captains of companies, frequently returned with very meager supplies, and, in three or four cases, without their commander, who had been assassinated, the men asserted, by the country people. Stringent orders were promulgated, a few examples were made, but to little purpose; the evil continued. At last, at the suggestion, it was said, of General Loison, the command of such parties was intrusted to the young officers. These, less severe than their seniors, and even occasionally winking at unavoidable infringements of orders, very generally returned to camp with abundance of provisions; in several such expeditions under my command, I never discovered that any of my men had been guilty of plunder, except for necessary food.

By a sort of tacit, mutual understanding, an intercourse, almost friendly, had established itself between the two armies, when not in actual conflict. At one particular point, the Tagus made a bend, formed by an island occupied by the English. From its

banks, English officers had frequently quite
amicable conversations with French officers,
on their bank of the river. If a British gun-
boat, unseen by us, came up the river, notice
was given us, and we retreated to war-
quarters. General Junot was once wounded
by neglecting such friendly warning. In all
cases, prisoners were treated by both nations
with commendable care and courtesy.

Sometime in February, 1811, my company
was at the outposts; our first lieutenant had
been out all night in search of provisions, and
instead of returning to the camp, found it
more convenient to stop first at our post, which
happened to be in his way. Among the booty
secured by his party was an old bull, an animal so rare as to become the object of unani-
mous acclamation by our party. Captain
Grignon, who commanded us, was so transported with joy, that not willing to leave to
another the honor of sacrificing the victim, he
snatched a musket from the stand of arms,
and hastily fired it into the animal's head.
The poor brute, which had not even been tied,

made a fearful leap forward, and galloped away, precisely in the direction of an English post, not visible from ours, but which we knew to be within half a mile. Without much hesitation, the following note was writ. ten in pencil, on the back of an envelop, viz: " Captain Grignon, 26th of the Line, presents compliments to the officer commanding the English post, and requests that he will return his bull." (This was certainly not a clear case of extradition, but our jolly captain was no casuist, and did not hesitate.) The laconic message was forthwith intrusted to a corporal and four men, in working undress, without arms, and immediately dispatched. It was then about eight o'clock A. M. Several hours passed without the re-appearance of our men, and the captain, being relieved at noon, was obliged to return to camp with the company, though beginning to indulge in sad misgivings in regard to his chivalric confidence in an enemy. On reaching the camp, instead of taking the rest which we badly needed, he and I returned to the outpost to satisfy our anxiety. No news had been received there about our stray men, and a vision of a court-martial began seriously to haunt the mind of the captain. However, about five o'clock P. M., we heard great huzzaing, which proceeded from the side of the English posts; forthwith, although it was almost dark, we saw about fifty red coats accompanying, with vociferous acclamations, our five soldiers, who preceded their enthusiastic escort, and who, drunk as Bacchus, were running tacks from one side of the road to the other, while yet seeming to join lustily in the outbursts of their excited new comrades. The English stopped as soon as they came within range of our sentries, and returned to their own quarters, after shaking hands heartily with our men. The latter at last reached us, and threw down their load, consisting of sundry pieces of beef, several loaves of bread strung on a rope, and two skins full of wine. As to explanations, we found it vain to extract any from them. They could utter nothing but drunken shouts to the honor and glory of the

English, who had treated them like princes, in the way of drink especially. We were forced to leave them at the post, to sober themselves by sleep. It was not until the next day that the corporal bethought himself of presenting to the captain a note addressed to him, together with two or three English newspapers which he had the day before carefully concealed under his clothes. The note, written in tolerably correct French, ran in something like the following terms: "Major ——, of the —— regiment, presents his compliments to Captain Grignon, and regrets to have only a part of the bull to return, beef being a scarce article in his quarters. As a compensation, he begs acceptance of a few loaves of bread and a little wine." I was soon called upon to translate (a task I could better perform than that of conversing), such passages of the paper as referred to our army, or to the emperor, under such titles as Bony, Nap, Nappy, or similar abbreviations, by which, in these papers, he was uniformly designated. We were soon horrified by the degrading, and to us blasphemous epithets unsparingly attached to the name and character of our demi-god, and I found the greatest difficulty in softening expressions which I shuddered to translate. We were not at the end of our troubles. In the evening of this same day, Captain Grignon was summoned before the commander-in-chief, made to relate all the circumstances of the transaction, and was finally dismissed with a sound reprimand and a severe admonition for the future. The next day, an order of the day was read before all the corps of the army, denouncing severe penalties against any one guilty of receiving communications of any sort from the enemy, and of introducing such into our camps.

At last, the time came when we were obliged to retire with as good a grace as we could assume. The country, for twenty miles round, was thoroughly depleted of all resources; many of our men were dressed like Harlequins, and in one regiment (my own) 850 men had, not bad shoes only, but no

shoes at all. The only thing of which we
had a sufficiency was tobacco, a store of this
article having been somewhere unearthed,
and many, many a meal was taken on smoke!
The scarcity of ammunition was also a source
of uneasiness at head-quarters.

Our retreat began about the 10th of March,
1811. The English army had, meanwhile
received considerable reinforcements from
England, besides the thousands of volunteers
levied in Portugal; but it was abundantly
supplied with all requisites, whilst, as I said
above, we were in a state of almost absolute
destitution. However, as we showed a bold
front, and had repulsed several outpost skirmishes, we were not seriously molested, except on three occasions. The first was at
Liria. This town boasted of only one wide
street, through which our army had to continue its retreat. The enemy pressed closely
on our rear with a powerful artillery, while
ours was already far beyond Liria. There
was but one resource left us. Orders were
given to the last column, and as they left the

above-mentioned street, they set fire to both
sides of it, and the enemy had the mortifica-
tion of seeing us quietly reach the position
previously appointed.

At the passage of the Mondego, a circumstance occurred similar to one more disastrous
that happened at Leipsic, three years later.
A sergeant of artillery, who had been left at
the bridge with orders to blow it up after all
the retreating army had crossed, became so
confused that he set fire to the mine when
a considerable number of men were still on the
enemy's side of the river. At Leipsic, the
unhappy blunder caused the death of a hero,
Prince Patowsky, and the capture of several
thousand men. On the Mondego, a part of
the thirty-sixth regiment was cut off, and a
whole convoy of mules abandoned to the
enemy.

At Sabugal, near the frontier of Spain, we
had a smart engagement, as if to bid a cordial
farewell to our British escort; and, to our
great satisfaction, we re-entered Spain, where
we found comparative abundance of supplies,

and, what was not to be despised, ten months'
pay, then due us.

We had hardly reached Salamanca when
information was received that Lord Wellington had invested Almeida, our last hold on
Portugal.   Back again we had to go by
forced marches, and once more confronted the
enemy on the third of May, 1811, at a village
called Fuentes D'onores, in the vicinity of
Almeida.   This was a memorable day for me,
as it influenced all my subsequent life by ar-
resting my fond aspirations after promotion
in a military career.

I was, during the greater part of the day,
engaged *en tirailleurs*, and at night was placed
with forty men at an out-post.   During the
night General Loyson came to the post, accompanied by a single aid.   He ordered me
to take out twenty men, and to lead him in
the direction which I thought likely to dis-
cover the nearest English posts.   We went
on stealthily for about half an hour, when the
general told me that I was probably mistaken
in my surmises, and that he was going to re-

turn to the camp. He, however, desired me to proceed for some time further, instructing me in case I should be challenged or fired at by a foreign vedette, not to answer, but to run back with my men to our post, and send word to head-quarters.

The night was very dark, and a drizzling rain was falling; our silent march was now on a narrow road, flanked by a hedge on either side. The general had not left us ten minutes when, on reaching an opening of the road, a perfect avalanche of blows overwhelmed my unlucky party in about the space of one minute. Not a shot was fired, the bayonet and the butt ends of muskets alone did the work, and strange to say, although all were more or less wounded, only one man, who had formerly been a drummer, was killed outright. As for myself, before I could well guess into what a wasp's nest I had fallen I was laid prostrated by a blow on the head, and with a slight bayonet or sword wound in my left shoulder. When I recovered my senses, for I had fainted, I found myself lying

on the grass, and surrounded by red coats.
A gentleman, whom I afterwards learned
was Sir Charles Stewart, addressed me in excellent French, and in very soothing terms.
Soon a surgeon made his appearance, and declared that the worst harm had been the blow
on the head, and that a few days would see
me well. I then learned that I had fallen into a post composed of two whole companies;
that my advance had been detected several minutes before the onset; and I was
thankful that General Loyson had been so
well inspired as to part with me when he did.
Being sent to the rear, I met in the hospital,
at Celorico, an officer whom the day before I
had observed falling from our desultory fire;
he had received a ball in his knee, from which
resulted permanent lameness; his acquaintance became valuable to me later on. His
name was A. H. Pattison, of Glasgow, and he
was, I believe, a captain in the 74th Regiment.

At Lisbon, where I arrived a few days later,
I had an unexpected and agreeable meeting.
As we, prisoners of war, escorted by a de-

tachment of infantry, were about to enter Fort Belleim, our destination until our embarkation for England, we met a number of English officers loitering near the gate of the fort. One of them approaching us suddenly gazed at the number on my shako, then on the buttons of my uniform, and thereupon called out excitedly to his comrades, who soon crowded round us. It turned out that these gentleman were officers of the 26th Regiment, British infantry, which formed at this time the garrison of Fort Belleim. They asked and obtained leave to keep me in their quarters during my detention there, and commenced their kind acts of hospitality by making me, at their mess, gloriously forgetful of my captivity, and of all other ills of this nether planet. A few days of this mode of life, altogether new to me, soon proved prejudicial to my health, and the regimental doctor declared that a continuation of such diet would soon consign me to Portuguese soil. The fact was, that the weather being very hot, the unaccustomed potations and high living

began to tell seriously on the wound in my
shoulder, and I had once more to be an
inmate of the hospital. Here I met again my
quondam friend, Captain Pattison, who, although much more grievously wounded than
myself, yet contrived to show me every attention in his power. Not the least of these was
to obtain for me a berth on the ship in which
he returned to England, instead of in one
specially allotted to prisoners of war. I was
then quite recovered in health, and had a very
pleasant voyage of ten days to Portsmouth.
I fared well on the passage, a quantity of delicacies having been sent on board for me by
my over-hospitable entertainers of the 26th
Regiment.

All the prisoners, numbering about sixty,
were landed at Gosport, a small town situated
on the western side of the bay, opposite
Portsmouth, and in which was established
the principal dépot of French soldiers, prisoners of war. Here, an unexpected pleasure
awaited me. Nearly two years previously I
had persuaded my nurse, who lived in a vil-

lage ten leagues from Paris, to allow one of her sons, my foster-brother, to enlist into my own regiment. The conscription was sure to overtake him before many months, and he would probably be assigned to a regiment, in which, having no friends, his life would not be a very easy one. He joined our corps, and at my request, was attached to my company. Proving to be a very intelligent cheerful young man, he soon became a favorite both with officers and men, and, being a sort of model soldier, had every prospect of rising in his profession. On the evening of the battle of Busaco, at roll call, I was dismayed beyond expression at his not answering to his name. I had seen and spoken to him several times during the day, but, in the confusion that followed, I had lost sight of him. The painful task of announcing his probable death to his mother devolved upon me; I, however, expressed a faint hope of his having been taken prisoner.

We, the officers, were quartered temporarily in a separate building, and were allowed, on our parole, to walk about the town. Our first impulse was to go and look at and converse with our countrymen, many of whom had already been for years in captivity. Here truth and justice compel me to combat an erroneous belief in regard to the harsh treatment of prisoners of war, which was propagated with a purpose at the time, and upheld by those of our men who were so unfortunate as to be confined in the *pontons—id est*, vessels out of commission, at anchor in the roads. There, indeed, they had a hard fate to bear: wretched food, little exercise extremely strict and occasionally cruel discipline—such was their lot; but we ascertained that none were sent to the *pontons* but refractory and incorrigible disturbers of the peace at Gosport prison; and also the crews of privateers indiscriminately, as the British government deemed such as having been captured in an illegal mode of warfare.

Whilst walking round the wooden palisade (a *clair-voie* surrounding the vast prison, which contained then upwards of five thou-

sand men, guarded outside by two regiments
of militia) I was suddenly startled by a loud
exclamation of: "Mon lieutenant! Mon lieutenant!" Those who were with me turned
round hastily, when the same voice reiterated :
" Mon lieutenant!" adding my name. I have
seldom experienced more exquisite joy than I
did then on recognizing my foster-brother,
looking well and hearty. After shaking
hands cordially with him through the trellis,
I called on the commander of the prison, and,
stating my case, solicited and obtained leave
to spend the day inside the prison. A prison
it was in reality, but resembling in all respects
a huge collection of barracks where an ad-
mirable organization had been established,
with strict yet humane regulations. Here, no
moans of despair were heard, no despondent
looks observable on the countenances of the
inmates, but on all sides resounded shouts of
laughter, or snatches of patriotic songs. This
philosophical making the best of things might
in part no doubt have been attributed to the

happy disposition of my countrymen—long
may they cherish it!

I was led by my foster-brother to a snug
little corner occupied by himself and a com-
rade, containing an apparently good bed, and
other small articles of furniture, partly purchased with their own money. The next
compartment was a kitchen, common to two
hundred men, and from which exhaled odors
not in the least indicative of a famished population. I remained to dinner. I shall not
say that the repast was sumptuous, but it was
abundantly supplied with good food; and, although served on pewter plates and dishes,
with knives and forks to match, it was seasoned with such cordial hospitality that the
remembrance of that dinner has ever left a
pleasant impression on my memory. Wine
or alcholic liquors were not produced, such
articles being excluded from the prison;
yet we were not restricted to cold water, for
we had a sufficiency of such excellent ale as is
manufactured in England alone. Amazed as
I was at this display of comfort in such a

place, one of my first questions was respecting the source of a degree of opulence for
which I could not account. This is the information which I received from my host.
He was the son of a basket maker, and himself knew something of the business. On arriving at the prison he availed himself of the
permission, liberally given to prisoners, to
work at such trades as they might be familiar
with, and to sell the produce. Customers
were numerous, owing to the cheapness and
to the general good quality of the prisoners'
work. This trade, however, had to be abandoned, from the extreme difficulty of procuring
material. But straw, in sufficient quantities,
was furnished to our men for bedding. Germain L——, after receiving instructions from
his fellow-captives, turned his ingenuity to
the manufacture of straw hats and bonnets,
and soon realized more money than his father
could earn at home. But, alas! this prosperity
was of short duration. The straw hat and bon-
net manufacturers of Portsmouth, and some
even of London and Barnstable, joined in an

earnest petition to the Transport Board,* for
the purpose of putting an end to a traffic
which very seriously affected their interest.
A total prohibition of such manufacture was,
in consequence, issued in the prison. Germain was not discouraged. He soon learned
another trade by forming a partnership with
one already skilled in the business; this was
the manufacturing bones into work-boxes,
combs, various kinds of toys, but especially
boats and ships. Material was abundant; a
sort of market was held twice a week, at
-which the different messes in the prison sent
all the bone they could collect; and a smart
competition among the manufacturers gave
rather a high value to these bones. My fos-
ter brother showed me a frigate, fully rigged,
upon which he was then at work, which cost
him and his partner six months' assiduous la-
bor, and for which, I was afterwards informed,
they obtained the handsome sum of forty

* The Transport Board was a government commission, to which the care and control of the prisoners of
war had been delegated. Its principal agents were officers in the British navy.

pounds sterling ($200). The cordage and
sails were constructed of human hair, collected in the prison. When he was liberated,
at the peace in 1814, he carried back to France
about one hundred and thirty pounds ($650),
the fruit of his industry. Here he bought a
small farm, married, and was much esteemed
among the inhabitants of his district. Poor
rich man! He died of the cholera in 1832. In
his conversation he never alluded to the period
of his captivity, without expatiating in glow-
ing terms on the integrity and liberality
evinced towards him by all the English, with
whom he had dealings. Such reports, and
many similar ones, circulated through France,
tended to weaken the keen feeling of hatred
and antagonism, to which war had given rise
between the two nations.

I have dwelt, perhaps, too long on this epi-
sode of my life, as it may possibly be devoid
of interest to my readers; it was far otherwise with me, and I felt almost compelled to
consign here this tribute of affection to the
memory of my foster-brother, Germain Lamy.

Repaying abundantly to me, whilst in captivity, any little services which it had been in my power to render him when with the regiment, could I not justly apply in this case the encouraging exhortation of Holy Writ, "Cast thy bread upon the waters, for thou shalt find it after many days?"

After a few days' stay at Gosport, I was, along with several others transferred, on parole to Odiham, a small town in Hampshire; there nothing occurred worth recording. The number of prisoners-of-war having been, about this period, considerably augmented by the taking of the Isle of France, Martinique, and Guadaloupe, the towns appointed to receive officers on parole in England proper, were found to be so inconveniently crowded that the government decided to quarter a portion of our number in Scotland, where none had hitherto been sent. (Political reasons precluded Ireland from having any share in the distribution of prisoners.) Odiham furnished its contingent, and I was one of the party thus transported

to Caledonia, where we landed at Leith, on
the 1st of October, 1811. From Edinburgh
we started for our destination, Selkirk, the
county town of Selkirkshire, thirty-six miles
south of Edinburgh. On the way, we halted
a few hours at Penay, where about two thousand of our soldiers and sailors were confined: the organization and regulations of
the prison appeared to us modeled on those
we had admired at Gosport.

Selkirk is situated on the river Ettrick,
which flows from the west and empties
itself into the Tweed, about half a mile from
the town. Few of its houses were covered
with slate; thatch being predominant. Its
population amounted to about two thousand
inhabitants, and although previous notice had
been given, we found, at first, some difficulty
in procuring lodgings for the hundred and
ninety men that constituted the new colony.
Matters soon altered in this respect; the people of the town found presently that we were
cash customers, and they vied with each other
in obtaining among us occupants for such of

their apartments as they could dispose of. Pleasant hills encircled the town on all sides; a pretty large square and a fountain occupied its center; a fine bridge spanned the Ettrick. A plain edifice belonging to the Church of England, and a much larger one owned by the Presbyterians, or rather a sect denominated "Anti-burghers," of whom a venerable, excellent man, named Laroun, was the pastor, were the only buildings worthy of notice in Selkirk.

Our pecuniary means were not ample, but were sufficient, every thing being remarkably cheap as compared with England. Our pay for all ranks, indiscriminately, was half a guinea (about three dollars) a week, regularly paid by the agent every Saturday morning. Besides, the majority of us received more or less money from France, through Th. Coutts, the London banker, who had been selected for this purpose by both governments. One of our number, named Belleville, was wealthy, and received annually about £1,000. My allowance from my family, paid quarterly, was £50. Altogether, we spent weekly about £150, so that when peace took place in 1814, that is, in the course of two years and a half, we had expended no less a sum that over £4,000, which was quite a consideration in such a small town, without trade or manufactures. In regard to our lodgings, we each paid, on an average, sixty cents a week; we generally clubbed together in a mess of from two to six members. Some of us became very fond of fishing, and successful in the pursuit, the Ettrick and Tweed abounding in trout and eels of excellent quality, as well as a lake in a neighboring mountain in very delicate pike. We were never molested in this sport, which proved a valuable resource in our culinary establishments.

We were too truly French to allow of our feelings being so utterly depressed by our captivity and the uncertainty of our relief as to make us pine away in useless sorrow or lamentations. A person captured at Martinique succeeded in passing himself off as a naval officer, and was accordingly admitted to his parole; he was one of our Selkirk colony, and possessing some pecuniary means, he procured from Edinburgh a billiard table, and all the requisites for establishing a very good coffee-house, to which no admittance was granted, except to our nationality. Soon after, ascertaining that some of us had received musical instruction, we rented instruments from the Capital, and mustered twenty-two efficient performers, who, under the leadership of a very superior violinist, constituted an orchestra superior to any that had ever resounded among the echoes of our Scottish residence. We invited to our concerts, gratuitously, of course, some of the inhabitants with whom we had become acquainted.

These recreations did not long satisfy our native activity. We collected among ourselves a sum of £100, rented a barn in the town, purchased a considerable quantity of lumber, as also necessary tools, and proceeded to construct a theater, etc.; and also benches sufficient for the accommodation of two hundred spectators. The orchestra was supplied by our band, already alluded to. The costumes, especially those for female characters, puzzled our ingenuity not a little; none of us had ever been a practical carpenter, upholsterer, tailor, or—apprentice to a dressmaker. Intelligence, however, stimulated by will, may perform small miracles. After several careful rehearsals, we had a select repertory drawn from our most popular tragic or comic authors, besides the partly musical works of our best vaudevillists. Every Wednesday we had a representation, to which we gave the same invitations as for the concerts on Saturdays, and our barn was usually crowded, though mostly with our own people.

On each of the four roads that converged into the town, and at the distance of one mile, a stone post was planted, and on it was painted the words: "Limit of the prisoners of war." A wag among us rooted up one of these stones, carried and transplanted it a mile further, to the amusement of the town's people, who, to their credit be it told, never in one instance availed themselves of a regulation in virtue of which any person who could swear that he had seen any of us beyond the appointed limit was entitled to receive from the culprit one guinea as a fine. I have repeatedly gone fishing several miles down the Tweed, without ever being fined, or in any way molested.

We had no society in the town, for before our arrival, the few persons who might claim rank as the gentry of the place had, as we understood later, concluded at a meeting held for the purpose, that they would not admit any of us into their circle. We were perfectly independent of their hospitality, and sneered at the absence of it. Advances, however, were made by some of the canny Scotch people in favor of Belleville, whose name I have already mentioned; the reason of this preference, of which he invariably declined to avail himself, was his being known to be very wealthy. However, we made a few pleasant acquaintances in the vicinity. Few of us will have forgotten the kind attentions which we received from Mr. Anderson, a gentleman farmer, who never seemed more pleased than when he could allure to and entertain in his home those of us who were enjoying the sport of fishing in the river on the banks of which stood his residence. Another friend of ours was a wealthy, retired lawyer, a *bon vivant* in the full sense of the term, and whose only fault, in our estimation, was his manifest chagrin when we did not keep pace with himself in the copious libations with which he regaled us. A third kind friend was a Mr. Thorburn, also a gentleman farmer, a most cordial host, who seemed bent on making his French guests acquainted with such Scottish delicacies as a grilled sheep's head, haggis, hodge-podge, and a splendid kind of cheese, of his own manufacture.

But there was one person whom I met at this time, the honor of whose acquaintance I did not then appreciate as I should have done in later years. Sir Walter Scott was then plain Mr. Scott, no one, except perhaps his publishers, even suspecting him to be " The

Great Unknown," author of Waverly.   As to
us, we saw in Mr. Scott only the sheriff of
Selkirkshire, and a lawyer of some repute in
Edinburgh.   In the former capacity, he frequently visited Selkirk, when at home at his
residence at Melrose Abbey, about three miles
distant from us.

Mr. Scott became acquainted with one of
our number, named Tarnier, a young man of
great talent, excellent education, and remarkable gayety of disposition.   Soon, without
the supposed knowledge of the government
agent, or rather with his tacit approbation,
Tarnier was invited to Melrose Abbey, and
gave us grand accounts of his reception there.
Presently, and probably at the suggestion of
our compatriot, he was authorized by Mr.
Scott to bring with him three of his friends
at each invitation to dinner at Melrose.   Thus
I was present on two or three occasions, invited, not by the host himself, but by my
friend Tarnier.

The period of the year was, to the best of
my remembrance, about February, 1813, and

our mode of proceeding was something like the following: Towards dusk, we, the guests, repaired to the mile-stone already mentioned; there a carriage awaited us, and soon conducted us to Melrose Abbey, where we were politely greeted by our host. We only saw Mrs. Scott for the few moments which intervened before dinner was announced, as she was not present at the repast. Mrs. Scott was, we understood, either a native of France, or of French parentage; at least, she spoke our language perfectly; Mr. Scott had married her at Berlin. Our host appeared to us in quite a different light from what we had seen of him in the streets of Selkirk. There, he impressed us as having a good-humored, rather coarse and unmeaning physiognomy, and awkward, almost vulgar walk and attitudes; this last, perhaps, owing to his lameness. At Melrose Abbey, we found him a cordial, cheerful gentleman, delicate in his kind attentions to his guests. The apartments were roomy and well-lighted, and the table, if not sumptuously, was at least ele-

gantly, furnished. It need not be expected
that I shall give here an elaborate description
of the surroundings of the mansion; on both
occasions of my visits, we arrived in the
dusky twilight, and departed amidst the dark
shades of night, by the same conveyance that
had brought us. Thus, with the exception
of the dining-room, and a glimpse of the par-
lor, all I know of Melrose Abbey I have derived from descriptive publications, which
any one may read. Neither can it be expected that I shall give any detail of repasts
of which I partook some sixty-five years ago.
But the general tenor of the conversation is
fixed immutably in my remembrance. Our
leading topic was not general politics, but
minute details connected with the French
army, and above all, traits and anecdotes
respecting Napoleon seemed to have an ab-
sorbing interest for our host, who, we re-
marked, incessantly contrived to lead back
the conversation to the subject, if it happened
to have diverged from it. As may be imag-
ined, we took care to say nothing unfavora-

ble to the character and honor of our beloved emperor. Little did we suspect that our host was then preparing a work, published ten years later, under the title of "A Life of Napoleon Bonaparte." In this unfair production, which is a stain on the name of its otherwise illustrious author, Sir Walter Scott relates anecdotes and circumstances connected with the emperor, many of which were communicated to him by us, but taking care to accompany each recital with sarcastic inuendoes, and self-invented motives of action, derogatory to the honor of Napoleon. The following is an instance :

During the armistice that followed the battle of Zurich, Prince Souwaroff and General Masséna spent several days in cordial and even familiar conversation in the Italian language. On one such occasion, the Russian general, alluding to certain confiscations of objects of art which had been sent to France, concluded by saying, "Tutti Francesi sono ladroni !" "Oh !" exclaimed Masséna, "tutti ??" "Tutti no, forse," replied

Suavaroff, smiling, "tutti no, ma buona parti."[1]—(Bonaparte.) This witticism, singular indeed as coming from a man known for the rude sternness of his character, and related to Sir Walter by one of us at his table, was seized upon by him as an occasion to avail himself of an authority so great as that of the renowned Russian general, in order to vilify Napoleon by representing him as an insatiable robber; whereas it is notorious that all the objects of art which he took from foreign countries, and especially from Italy, were previously estimated as to their value by a committee composed partly of Italians, and received, not stolen, in lieu of payment of the war indemnities levied on the country. Moreover, it is admitted on all hands, that Napoleon, conveying these treasures to France, never allowed any of them to be placed in his residences as his own private property, but invariably distributed them among the National Museums of Paris and other cities.

---

[1] "All Frenchmen are robbers." "Oh! all?" "All, no, but a good part."—(Bonaparte.)

Thus passed and ended my brief acquaintance
with an illustrious character.

Our friendly intercourse with the worthy
inhabitants of Selkirk was interrupted only
on two occasions, rather amusing than serious, but which might have become tragical.

On the 15th of August, 1813, we met at a
banquet, intended as a celebration of the emperor's birthday. Our coffee-room was the
place of meeting; it was on the ground-floor,
with windows opening on the public square,
and at the outside corner of the building was
a narrow lane leading to the rear of the town.
About one hundred of us were present, although we had provided for double that number. The dinner passed off very pleasantly,
and after numerous toasts had been disposed
of, accompanied by songs, speeches, and acclamations, it was observed that the table
still remained loaded with a large quantity
of eatables, which we could not consume. It
was suggested that the proper use to be made
of these good things was to distribute them
among the populace, who, by this time, had

collected in crowds on the square. To this
suggestion, which was unanimously approved,
was added another, which was carried by acclamation; this amendment consisted in our
requiring that each applicant for our bounty
should, previous to his receiving it, take off
his hat and shout, "Vive l'Empereur Napoleon!" Accordingly, several of us posted
ourselves at the entrance of the lane before
mentioned, bearing in one hand half a ham,
turkey, or roast beef, etc., and in the other
a tumblerful of wine, brandy, or whisky.
The difficulty was to induce our pseudo
guests to comply with our *sine qua non* condition; all hesitated and held back. Finally,
we perceived among the crowd a man who
served us as a kind of factotum, and who, in
this capacity, made a great deal of money by
us. This person, whose real name I never
knew, had been nicknamed Bang-bay, from
the following circumstances: constantly tor-
mented by simultaneous calls for his services,
his usual impatient reply was, By-and-by.
This expression, not understood by most of

us, was changed into Bang-bay, which was
the nearest approach we could make towards
pronouncing it, and he was always known
amongst us by that euphonious appellation.
As having therefore some authority over this
man, we called upon him to come forward;
he obeyed, and, after a short hesitation, complied with our condition, received nearly a
whole roast turkey, quaffed a brimful tum-
bler of liquor, and was then dismissed, not
back to the square, but through the lane to
the rear of the town. From that moment
our only difficulty lay in supplying the numbers who pressed forward as candidates for
drinking the glorious toast. Soon our supplies gave out, and the loudly expressed dis-
satisfaction of those who had hitherto only
been spectators of the fun gave us infinite
satisfaction. It was not to be of long duration. The crowd had slowly dispersed, but
half an hour later they again assembled in
the square. We had resumed our seats, and
were listening to a song composed for the
occasion, when a stone, thrown through the

window, struck a captain of artillery named
Gruffand. Instantly he sprang out of the
window, and addressing the mob in impe-
rious tones, demanded, "What rascal among
you threw that stone?" All kept silent; but
seeing a sneer on the countenance of one
of the mob, he continued, "Perhaps *you*
did; you who are making faces over there?"
"Perhaps I did," answered the young man
boldly. Hardly had he uttered the words,
when Gruffand hurled the stone right in his
face, wounding him severely. A tumult was
about to ensue, when our attention being
drawn to the scene, we seized knives and
forks, broke a few chairs to serve us as staves,
and sallied forth through the doors and windows, to the rescue of our friend. The people
being unarmed, thought it best not to test our
weapons, but at once deserted the square. A
little later, however, the agent, Mr. Robert
Henderson, came hurriedly to give us notice
that a new mob was organizing with arms, and
that the matter might become very serious;
that, moreover, we were in one respect in the

wrong, as it was now ten o'clock, whereas by the
regulations which we had engaged implicitly
to obey, we should have been in our respective
lodgings by nine o'clock. We admitted at once
the reasonableness of these observations, and
retired without molestation. The affair had no
sequel, and both parties shortly resumed better
feelings towards each other.

Soon, however, we conceived we had another and more serious cause of displeasure.
Upon the announcement of a victory of Wellington in Spain, the people of Selkirk had
the bad taste, if not the indelicacy, considering
our position, to ring all the bells in the town,
and to display an extravagant and insulting
joy. We were not long in retaliating. Not
many days had passed when, one Saturday,
news arrived of a great victory gained by the
French army in Russia. Our plans were soon
arranged. The following day being Sunday,
two of our party attended the service at the
meeting house, and they contrived to secrete
themselves in such a manner that the doors
were closed on them without their being dis-

covered. At midnight the watchers unbolted one of the windows, and admitted half a dozen of their confederates; these last had provided themselves with a long rope, which was soon fastened to the one attached to the bell. Six stout arms soon developed all its sounding notes, to the imminent danger of cracking the instrument, and, in a few minutes, wonder and consternation spread through the town. Before the crowd, which ran from all quarters, had collected at the church, our party had escaped to their quarters, secure from fear of discovery. Although suspicion strongly pointed our way, nothing could be proved against us, and the affair was dropped.

At last peace was proclaimed, and we were notified that a vessel would be ready at Berwick, on the 26th of April, 1814, to convey us to Boulogne or Calais. I need hardly say with what transports of joy this news was received by us; a joy which I suspect was not shared by those whose lodgings were now to be left vacant.

The few of us who had sufficient pecuniary means proposed to go in carriages to Ber. wick; but at a general meeting convened for the purpose, it was proposed by Belleville that all the money we possessed should be merged into one common fund, and distributed equally *per capita*, so that all should go on the same footing; he himself gave the example by contributing all he had on hand, about £30. The whole sum thus collected not amounting to more than about £60, we concluded that we should all take the journey together, and on foot; one old colonel, and two other officers in ill health, were alone exempted from this arrangement, and a carriage was provided for them.

We had one anxiety in leaving Selkirk, namely, the fear of departing without enjoying another bit of fun; an opportunity, however, presented itself, and we were not disposed to reject it. The materials for our theater, consisting of boards, seats, decorations, costumes, etc., had cost us about £120; the work itself cost us nothing, we being our own

carpenters, smiths, painters, tailors, etc. These
materials would, in our estimation, provide
us with the means of performing our journey more comfortably. Accordingly, we announced that the next day we should sell said
lumber, etc., by auction at our barn; one
witty young officer, Tarnier, who spoke English fluently, was to act as auctioneer. At
the time appointed, the attendance was large,
and looked very encouraging. The starting
price was announced to be £50, but soon had
to be reduced to £20. From this point,
amidst the expostulations of the auctioneer,
answered by sneers from a part of the audience, the highest bid offered amounted to
£4! We soon had an understanding among
ourselves. Our worthy auctioneer announced
to the assembly that the barn being too confined, we should proceed with the auction in
a field contiguous to the town, and hitherto
rented by us for foot-ball exercise. With
promptitude, and accompanied by the noisy
merriment of the crowd, we shouldered boards,
benches, etc., and conveyed them to the new

scene of operation. But so careful were we
of our neat decorations, scenery, and costumes, that we first laid under them a quantity of straw, and then surmounted the whole
with a high pile of lumber. The auction was
now resumed, and Tarnier's voluble eloquence
was exerted to the utmost to strike any chord
of liberality that might slacken a little the
purse strings of our Scottish friends. All in
vain; the latter knew that the things *must* be
sold, and the highest obtainable bid was £6.
A few of us, well provided with steel, flints,
and *amadou* (tinder), were posted round the
mass of inflammable material; at a precon-
certed signal from our auctioneer, the pile
burst into a blaze, to the great danger of set-
ting fire to the town, had there been a wind.
The bonfire was greeted by us with hearty
shouts of "Vive l'Empereur," although we
knew that he had already abdicated, and by
mingled cries of disappointment and merriment from the crowd of astonished by-
standers.

At last the day of our final departure arrived; Tuesday morning was the time appointed. Most of us had passed the night on the square, singing and merry-making, so we were all ready, and were about starting, when a new and pleasant sight met our view. Vehicles of all descriptions were seen pouring down the two principal streets leading to the town—carriages, gigs, wagons, and a few saddle horses; these had been sent by the inhabitants of the neighborhood to convey us free of expense as far as Kelso, about half way to Berwick. This liberal attention was so well timed and so delicately performed that we could not do otherwise than avail ourselves of it with many thanks, and thus we parted from our Kelso friends without entertaining, on either side, any remnant of grudge that might previously have existed between us.

On arriving at Boulogne, our feelings were sorely tried at perceiving our beloved tricolor replaced on all public buildings by the hated white flag; this unpleasant sensation was intensified a little later by an outrage which aroused all our ill-disposed sentiments.

We had landed about ten o'clock in the morning, and had been directed to the mayor's office, where we were to receive our lodging billets. At four in the afternoon we were still standing or sitting on the pavement in the street awaiting the convenience of his honor, the mayor, a recently returned emigrant. Unfortunately for myself, I happened to be near the office door when it finally opened, and no sooner had I passed the threshold than I poured forth a torrent of indignant reproach on the mayor, and, among other sarcasms, told him that under the *emperor* he dared not have conducted himself thus shamefully towards French officers returning from captivity. The altercation was cut short by the interference of some of my more cautious friends, but we observed that the mayor took notes, as we rightly conjectured, of my name, and the number of my regiment.

A few days later, I arrived at Paris, and proceeded to the war office to take further orders, first handing, as usual, my card to the

usher. Many others were before me, probably on the same errand; but when at last
my name was called, I was introduced into the
private office of an elderly officer, wearing the
uniform of a general. Before I had time to
state my case, he asked me when and where I
had landed from England; on my answer, he
addressed me without hesitation, not a warning—that should have been sufficient, in consideration of my youth, and the position I
held—but a severe reprimand, which he concluded by desiring me to leave my address in
the lower office. I left in a high state of indignation. Once at home, my first care, in spite
of all the entreaties of my friends, was to
write in the curtest terms my resignation, and
to carry it immediately myself to the war
office. By evening of the same day I received the answer, "Your resignation is accepted."

Thus ended, for that time at least, my experience of life in the army.